The Legend of the School Ghost

Written and Illustrated By

Olivia Henderson

"The Revenge of the School Ghost," published through Young Author Academy.

Young Author Academy

Dubai, United Arab Emirates

www.youngauthoracademy.com

ISBN: 9798759732136

Printed by Amazon Direct Publishing.

To my family, I hope you love this book
as much as I love you all.

To Annemieke, thank you for all your support and
guidance. I could not have done this without you.

To my sisters, Poppy and Annalise,
thank you for being my inspiration.

To Mum and Dad,
thank you for believing in me
that I could write this book.

Hi, I am Maple Huston.

This is my story of the Revenge School Ghost…

Okay, I know what you're thinking?

…That I'm crazy, but I am NOT!

or that there was an invisible kid or both,
but I was very confident that it was a ghost.

Contents

- CHAPTER ONE -

Maple's Theory

Once there was a young girl called Maple. Maple attended Hoovington High. She thought, in fact she just knew, that there was a ghost that haunted the school. She was convinced of it.

Maple had a theory.

She thought that the ghost chose her high school to haunt, because it just didn't like children. Maple believed that it wanted to get the school children into trouble. For instance, it would always leave behind a lot of foam soap on the bathroom sink bowl and also on the floor.

At first, Maple's teacher didn't really mind because it was a small bathroom at the back of the classroom and it only happened every few weeks, but then it would start to happen more often and there would be a bubble trail from the bathroom into the classroom every time someone went to the bathroom.

This behaviour got Maple's teacher angry. Then for some strange reason, it stopped for a few days, so her teacher thought that the students' bad behaviour had stopped but it turned out that the ghost was just planning revenge.

This is the story of how Maple tracked down and proved that there was a school Ghost...

- CHAPTER TWO -

Gathering Clues

It all started when.......

The revenge got so bad. So bad that it took a few days to plan. Maple hadn't noticed any pranking or actions from the ghost for a while, so she figured he might be planning his next revenge move. Maple thought they she needed to plan to stop him from his next move.

You know in the movies when there is a big evil plan with a bad guy in make up and superhero's just come and stop them in a split-second? Well, it was like that but there were no superheroes or bad guys, just a ghost and a little girl with her best friend. But that's enough about comics.

Back to the story....

Maple's plan was simple! She needed to clog the sink so that there were no bubbles.

I know what you're thinking! You're thinking that if it took a few days to plan then it had to be amazing, but it took a few days to plan because this was her only idea that was really possible. All of the others involved all sort of bits and bobs that didn't exist, like one of the ideas was to sneak to school on the weekend and wrap the ghost with a ghost suction-wrapper.

There were three things wrong with this plan! Can you guess?

Maple didn't have a ghost-suction wrapper. She didn't know what time the ghost would attack or if the ghost would at all, and lastly she couldn't sneak to school because it took her ten minutes just to reach school in the car. She couldn't drive, so that was off the small and pointless list.

One Thursday (the last day before the weekend or the day before when Maple thought that the ghosts may attack next), she clogged the drain with an old bottle lid that she got from a bottle that she had drank at lunch. She thought, 'that was it! And the ghost will stop its pranks,' she thought, but sadly, the ghost had other plans.

What Maple didn't realize was when it found out that the bathroom sink was clogged, it just simply went to the bathroom next to Maples' classroom with a bucket and used up all the soap in there. It made the biggest pile of soap that you could imagine.

If you are one of those people that want to know every little detail - the foam mountain was exactly 2.4 metres high, although this is a slight exaggeration.

The ghost went back to Maples' classroom and plugged the bathroom holes up until it couldn't be filled any more.

Two long days later, when the students had returned to school after a weekend, the teacher was in a bad mood. She had also run out of coffee, so she was in a very bad mood.

Maple wanted to see if her old bottle lid idea had done the trick, but if it was bad then Maple figured that she would be in a lot of trouble, so she asked Sam Harris, a student with typically very bad luck, if anyone had been in the bathroom.

He said a solid, 'No!'

Thoughts were racing through Maples' head; should she go in and take a look? or should she wait for someone to go in and find out themselves.

Then Robert, the gross boy in town, went over to Maple. She held her breath. He asked Sam if the cleaning lady had been. Obviously he said, 'No.'

Robert

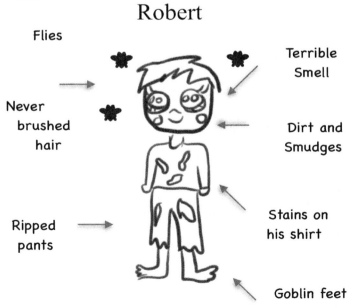

Flies

Terrible
Smell

Never
brushed
hair

Dirt and
Smudges

Ripped
pants

Stains on
his shirt

Goblin feet

Maple was so intrigued so she watched closely. She also noticed that the teacher was intrigued by now as she was looking towards the bathroom door, as if she knew what was going on. Robert opened the door and the whole bathroom was a foam blob.

This time Maple thought that the teacher would be super mad, except she said something rather surprising. "I'm so sorry class!" said the teacher calmly. "It wasn't any of you who has created the foam-mess, it was someone else, like the janitor, Gusto. He has been creeping me out! I will tell the Principal about this right away!" Then our teacher hurried off to the Principals' office.

We were all stunned! 'She finally knows that we didn't do it?' thought Maple.

Meanwhile, Mrs Pebble was in the queue waiting to see the Principal.

There was a line of children and teachers with them, but it was quite quiet today since there was only a boy waiting in line, in front of her.

About ten minutes later, the boy had been in to see the Principal and had since come out. The Principal was now free. Mrs Pebble and the Principal, Mr Walker, had a detailed discussion about how Gusto was super creepy and that they should question him.

After school, Gusto the janitor was called to the Principal's Office, where he was questioned, "Have you been putting foam all over my bathroom?" shouted Mrs Pebble in a terrifying voice. Even Mr walker was surprised by her tone.

"Kind of! Well, I mean I have been washing my hands in the sink and perhaps I am not so clean at washing my hands, so all of the soap sometimes end up on the sink bowl and floor," replied Gusto the Janitor.

"Please don't do it again. I have been blaming my students and I have also been punishing them for no reason at all."

And that was the stop to the foam problem in the school bathroom.

The next day was surprisingly nice. There was an hour of golden time; the funnest lessons in the world and that was all because Mrs Pebble felt bad about blaming the students.

- CHAPTER THREE -

The Case of the Extra Waxy Slide

There was no bathroom problem for a whole week. Now that was an achievement! But Maple thought that things were getting a little fishy, so every once in a while she would ask to go to the bathroom just to inspect it, very thoroughly for foam and bubbles. She would even check the drain for bubbles. The drain was the best place to check for foam because that was where the water normally goes after you wash your hands. It is also the place where the foam tends to explode. In the walls, deep in thought was a ghost thinking of his next prank, since his last one failed.

Little did Maple know that he had stolen the school map from the school reception. He thought of each place around the school that the kids would spend time, but none of them worked. Then he thought, 'The playground!' so he took out his playground map and studied it clearly.

The ghost thought that perhaps the swings was a good place to start, but there was no prank that he could pull because he liked the children that typically liked to go on the swings so much that he realized that he would never pull a prank there.

He then thought of the sandpit, but he didn't like sand getting inside of him. He thought of the monkey bars but he was scared of heights. He then suddenly thought....... THE SLIDE.

But there were two slides. The one he was thinking of in particular, was next to the recycling bins.

Hours later, after a long time thinking and pondering of some wonderful pranks that he could do, there was one that stood out. He decided to put wax in the caretakers bucket when they washed the slide, but to make it extra slippery, he was going to wax it at midnight when nobody was around, just to make sure he didn't get caught.

The next morning at seven thirty sharp, he heard the laughter and giggles of children as they entered the school gates. He could smell the fresh breeze and a hint of turkey, cheese and chip sandwiches wafting from the children's lunchboxes.

Every once in a while, he caught a waft of quinoa and red pepper salad with sesame dressing from the more health conscious children (but they were few and far between).

The ghost peeked around the corner at 8 o'clock sharp where he found the caretaker washing the slide, but little did he know that he was also waxing it.

Now, the ghost thought, 'the slide needs just one more layer before the kids come out at snack time to play.' As soon as Gusto, the janitor, was done cleaning the slide, the ghost rustled around in some trees and scared a flock of school pigeons towards the slide. They were so scared that they pooped all over it. The janitor shooed them away and got busy cleaning (and waxing) the slide once again.

That meant the three layers of wax were complete and all in time for it to set, ahead of break time.

The ghost waited impatiently in his secret lair, waiting for the time to pass by. He played with gadgets that he had previously stolen from the fidget confiscation box and he even had a short nap because he had been up all night putting his plan into action.

He did think however, 'Had he put enough layers on the slide?' So he decided that he needed to arrange for one more layer of wax to be applied to the slide. He needed to figure out how to do it though.

Putting one more layer on wasn't proving easy. "I can't make the cleaner wash it again," said the ghost to himself.

The ghost stood behind the bush nearest to the slide very scared, wondering, 'had he given it enough time for the wax to set?'

At the same time, Maple was again becoming very suspicious about when the ghost was going to strike again, so she planned to just have fun, as she had no idea of what was about to happen.

One minute later, all of the kids came out of their classrooms and into the play ground. Sammy Keys got to the slide first.

Remember Sammy Keys?
The unluckiest person in the school and if he ever got to the slide first, it would send a message to the other students that they should not follow, because then every body would know that something bad was about to happen.

Maple had a feeling (which was never good) that this had something to do with the ghost.

Sammy Keys went on about how he got to the slide first and all the things you would do to brag. He went down the slide and that's when the trouble started. As you all ready know, the ghost was in the bushes right next to the teacher that was watching them for break, but as soon as Sammy Keys pushed to go down the slide, he flew off the end like a rocket and splatted head-first into the gross eco-bin, that had banana peels in it.

The teacher was horrified that someone would actually want to do something like this. The ghost stood watching and was overjoyed with happiness.

The teacher made them all stand in a line and questioned them very carefully. Maple and Zach were at the end of the line. Since it took one minute to question each student, and there were sixteen in front of them, they had about ten minutes to figure out what had happened, or at least come up with some reason or excuse. There was no time to waste.

They set off and when they reached the slide, Maple smelt something unusual. Within a minute, she knew exactly what it was.

"That smell is wax, from my dads building supplies," stated Maple with a shocked face.

"Come on! There two more people to go," replied Zach.

They hurried back to the line with a minute spare, "NEXT!" shouted the teacher. "Do you know anything about the trouble?" As he pointed to the kids that were helping Sammy Keys out of the eco bin.

"Yes!" The teacher leaned in, "If you come to the slide, I will show you."

"Okay!" They moved to the slide. "What's that smell?" the teacher asked.

"The smell is wax and the someone must have put wax in the bucket that the janitor uses so that he could wax it without getting caught."

Without another word being said, he set off to the janitors office, took a sample of the water and then gave it to the science teacher to analyse. She did a quick examination. There was wax in it!

Mr Harrison, who was the playground monitor teacher, marched to the Principal and flung the door open. He explained what had happened and then he called the janitor in and asked him how many times he had washed the slide. It was four times. So they unwaxed it with cleaning agents and everything went back to normal, but Maple and Zach's suspicion grew even further.

"Why is the ghost doing these tricks?" queried Zach, "Do you think he trying to kill us?"

"I think he is just doing his job," replied Maple.

"What job? I'm confused. Ghost's don't have jobs!"

"No silly, a ghost's job is to haunt people that killed him," stated Maple.

It was very weird that Maple was telling a fact about ghosts to Zach.

"Bingo!" suddenly a thought came to Zach's mind. "The ghost died in this school!"

- CHAPTER FOUR -

The Heist

So the last two pranks had failed but it was getting pretty intense. His last two plans had failed, but the ghost was determined to drive the teachers mad. It looked like he would have to change his theory, from pulling a trick on the school to... well that was the problem... he couldn't figure out what he could change his theory to. You see the ghost had many different pranks but he didn't know if any of his ideas would work.

He planned to smash the wall in the science classroom because everyone hated science.

I know that you're thinking
that it was a perfect plan...
But this ghost ain't have any muscle,
so there would be no damage to the wall.

"Snap out of it! We need to find a new theory, not a prank," said the ghost to himself who was very frustrated and stumped. None of his theories were good but one did stand. Instead of pranking a place, he would ruin an event. There was only one problem with the prank! This ghost didn't know any events that were going to occur inside the school. He didn't know of any events that were being planned.

Suddenly, he heard some familiar voices. It was Principal Tampert and the Office Receptionist.

They happened to be talking about all events that were happening and listed in the school calendar. What good luck!

The ghost had an idea! He would create a wicked plan to steal the school calendar. He decided that he would plan to steal it at dawn.

The next day at dawn, he set off on his feet to steal the school calendar. He hopped on his scooter and scooted away.

Every once in a while he would have to climb the ladders on the side of the building to get on top of the roof, normally because security was coming.

As soon as reached the ladder, he hopped off the scooter and snuck in the back door, (where the teachers were only allowed to go) and floated to the reception desk and looked for this thing called 'The School Calendar'.

At last he had found it. It had a red border at the top and down the left side a lot of white squares with events written in them, and at the top in bold letters, was,

"THE SCHOOL EVENT CALENDAR"

As quiet as the speed of light, he darted onto his scooter, climbed onto the roof and back he went. Once he returned, he kicked the math display and climbed into the hole and entered his secret lair.

With a KABOOM! he fell face flat onto his bed, and collapsed he was so tired.

At last, he had taken the school calendar.

He flipped through it and was amazed to find out that the next event was in two days.

'Perfect! He had lots of time to plan,' the ghost thought. The only bad thing was that he had no idea what he could do for a football prank.

The next event was a football match. He had never done a football prank before.

But it was getting late, so he went to bed? Yes! He went to bed!

I know you're thinking, some people would think, 'but why is he sleeping?'
Well, otherwise, he would get really cranky.

The next day he got up pretty early so he could think of a prank that will ruin the event.

Nothing came to his mind. He had never pulled a prank at PE because there was nowhere to hide; no walls, no room that had furniture to hide behind and worst of all, the only one place to hide and that was the sun protector.

You might be thinking that it sounded like it was the best spot to hide;
the sun protector...

...Well you'd be wrong! It is the land of screams and pigeons, because as soon as a ghost stepped onto the dark, the birds fired his greatest weapon: His, but which is where the poop comes out.

The ghost thought hard about an idea, and then one finally came to him. It was to do something to the ball every time when someone kicked it, but the only thing that was missing, was his thought about what would happen when someone did kick the ball.

Suddenly, a thought came to his his mind, 'he could put spikes on the football team's shoes and then when they kicked the ball, it would pop, so all he had to do was put spikes on their shoes, without them knowing.'

- CHAPTER FIVE -

The Football Match

Maple had asked Zach to come over to her house after school. Zach headed to Maple's house, but when he was about to ring the doorbell, suddenly a bony and creepy hand grabbed him and pulled him into the bushes. It was Maple.

"What are you doing Maple? Can't I ring the doorbell?" exclaimed Zach.

"No!" replied Maple, "Remember my mum hates it when you come over to talk about the ghost."

"Then how are you supposed to get to your room, now?" demanded Zach.

"The rope silly. I tied it to the bed leg. Don't worry, it won't move," explained Maple. "Now come on, we have work to do." And with that, they climbed up the rope and clambered into Maple's bedroom.

Off they set, trying to find out the ghost was planning next. After ten minutes of hard thinking, Zach had an idea. "In ghostbusters, most of the time, the ghosts ruin events."

"BINGO! That is now! What is the next event that is planned?" said Maple.

"No! Did you forget that my football match is tomorrow?" stated Zach with concern.

"Of course, I have not forgotten, but maybe he will have a plan to ruin the football match!"

"The game? That way he can make us lose, but what?" said Maple, "What is he planning? We need to stop him!"

"Okay, but there's one problem," replied Zach. "I'm playing at the football!"

"Firstly, make sure everything is good on the inside of the football match."

"Okay, I can do that," said Zach.

Meanwhile, he had already stolen the teacher's camera and had taken a photo of the football team-board and ground-out where they were all. It was dark and it was time to start putting spikes on their shoes.

The ghost had already drawn a map.

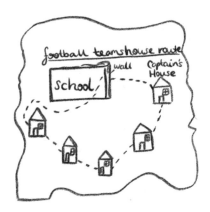

First, he went to the Captain of the football team and put spikes on his shoes. He repeated this for all of the footballers boots and the goalies gloves. He was done by about 3am and headed to his lair.

The team members didn't see the spikes. When they were putting on their shoes, they were focussed on the coach giving them instructions.

When it was time to start the game, Maple sat down on the bleachers just next the spot where the ghost was sitting.

"That's strange! The footballers have spikes on their shoes. I must let them know at half-time," said Maple.

But it was too late. The match had already begun. Bryan started the game with a big kick and whoosh and PFF!

Just as the referee was about to put the ball in the middle of the court, he felt that it was flat. So he did something strange. He asked the players around him, "Who can explain this flat ball?"

Suddenly, Maples' hand shot up and everyone was shocked. Maple shouted, as Zach was in shock. "No you silly! I know why the ball is flat."

Everyone was intrigued. "Someone put spikes on your shoes," pointing to their indeed, spiked shoes.

All Maple wanted to know was why a ghost would do this, but she knew it would have to make sense eventually. Then the coaches decided to just postpone the match to another day.

The Principal was becoming suspicious of all of these pranks that were happening in the school, and asked Maple if she could be a detective to investigate it a little more.

By the the next week, everything went back to normal.

- CHAPTER SIX -

The Glue in the Bun

Now the ghost was getting super angry. None of his pranks had worked and a detective was now onto him. So he decided to change his plans.

Again, he thought long and hard. At about 10:00am one morning a few days later, an idea came to his mind. 'If kids keep ruining my plans, then I'll prank somewhere that children can't go,' the ghost thought excitedly as he was hovering in the teachers lounge. Then he set towards putting his prank into action.

Meanwhile, Maple had been head detective for nearly a week and she wanted to catch the ghost in the act, but just didn't know how she wanted to be there when the ghost showed up. But first she needed to know where he was going to prank.

'Maybe now he had a workspace which was cleared. A storage room of sorts,' Maple thought to herself.

She thought hard and long for a good twenty minutes until suddenly something came to her. 'If we keep on ruining my pranks theme, he will eventually pull a prank, where kids can't go.'

Then another thought came to her mind... 'the teachers lounge!'

Of course, that was the best place to prank in the school. In his lair, the ghost had just thought of the perfect prank.

It was to put glue into the bread buns in the cafeteria.

Maple walked to the teachers lounge and hid under the table and waited for a while. Like she had suspected, a ghostly figure appeared. He was putting glue in the buns.

"I knew it!! Stop!" shouted Maple. "How dare you!"

The ghost froze and gasped. Still astonished, the ghost said, "How did you know I was going to be here?"

"I just assumed you would be," answered Maple.

"It's because kids keep ruining your plans so I thought you might go somewhere where kids can't go, and kids can't come to the teachers lounge!"

"Well that is true and you do keep ruining my plans but how did you know what time I would come here?"

"What are you doing anyway?"said Maple, ignoring his question.

"I am doing my prank, my best prank yet!" said the ghost proudly.

"I meant what is your prank?" said Maple, still very confused about the situation.

"I was putting glue in the teachers favourite sticky buns," he laughed, "so that when they take a bite, their mouths will be glued shut and they will be really angry at the children."

"You have answered one of my questions but what about the other? Who are you?" quizzed Maple.

"Well I am Gary the school's old janitor and my son Gusto took over my job when I died," explained the ghost.

Maple, still feeling very confused, asked, "Why are you pulling all of these pranks when you used to clean up all of them?"

"It's because I hate children and I am trying to get them in trouble so that they will go away."

"WHY?" Maple continued to query.

"Well! It all began when I was auditioning to be a teacher at this very school. I was about thirty years old then and I needed money and I got fired from my teaching job from another school," said the ghost. He went on to say, "They gave me a trial to take a detention class of five very bad kids who made the janitor quit. It all started well with them reading comics but I got them to start reading their science books, but it didn't take long for them to start chaos. Soon they had escaped from detention through the air vents and I found them hiding in the bathroom but they ran away. After ten minutes I tracked them down to the slide but they managed to escape again. I gave up looking for them after an hour of searching and went for a cup of tea and a sticky bun in the teacher's lounge."

"Hold up! Hold up! that explains the prank in the bathroom and on the slide, but what about the football match?" asked Maple.

The ghost replied, "Well I changed my strategy and that was the only event in the calendar and I wanted to make a big bang. Except, the five boys had gotten there first. They had already made a 'big bang' by putting glue in my sticky bun and this led to this very occasion!"

"Did you ever find them?" asked Maple, interrupting the ghost.

"Could you stop interrupting me! I had just taken a bite of the sticky bun when the five boys jumped out from behind a pot plant and shouted Got Ya! I was about to tell them to go back to detention but my mouth couldn't open to get the word out. It was glued shut."

"Then why are you doing the same thing to the teachers?" asked Maple.

"Well, it was so that the teachers would get mad and blame the students - like I have been trying to do for every other prank I have attempted to pull off," replied the Ghost.

Maple said with a knowing grin, "They know it is you. I am now the detective of the school and have already sent photos of you to the Principal Lampert. I have just sent him a text telling him that I have caught the prankster and he is coming over to deal with you."

The Ghost looked at Maple thinking she was silly. "How did you take a photo of me? You know that you cannot see a ghost in a picture?"

Maple looked at the photo that she had taken on her phone and realized the ghost was right. You couldn't see him at all in the photo that she had sent to Principal Lampert.

Knowing she had messed up, she quickly typed a message to the Principal reading, 'Just ignore that message. I was wrong!'

"So have you caught on now?" asked the Ghost. "I am a ghost and I hate children. I pull the pranks to try and get them in trouble."

"Wait! You said you wanted to scare them away right?" said Maple.

"I know I said that, but it doesn't work that way - it is a school. The children have to come here!" the Ghost replied.

Just in that moment, the Principal walked into the teacher's lounge room where Maple and the ghost was. Upon seeing the ghost 'in person', the Principal became very confused.

"Wait! You are not a student!" asked the Principal. He turned to Maple and asked, "Maple, what is this creature and is it by chance, the Prankster?"

Maple replied, "He is a ghost and he is the prankster, yes! He is responsible for all the pranks that have been happening in the school lately."

"Why?" the Principal asked the ghost. "What are you trying to achieve with these pranks?"

"Well, I hate children and I want to get them into trouble."

Maple gave him a stern look.

The Ghost continued, "..And to scare them away. I was a janitor at this school fifty years ago and the children teased me and played pranks on me. Now, I am getting my own back!" The ghost started laughing an evil laugh.

The Principal had a sudden realisation. "You are the person in the old tale who interviewed for a teaching role, let the children escape from detention and had to go to hospital because your mouth was glued shut. Was that you? From many years ago."

"YES!! That was me!" yelled the Ghost. "I am the teacher who had to become a janitor after that. That is why I wanted to play pranks on the children. I hate them!"

The Principal felt sorry for the ghost. "What happened to you back then was terrible. We want to make sure that that never happens to any teachers or students again. I have an idea! I think you would make a great teacher's assistant, working with Maple to stop any pranks taking place at this school in the future. Would you be prepared to do this? In exchange, we will let you stay in the school."

"That sounds like a great idea. I really do like haunting Hoovington High school - and I could now continue doing it, for a good reason," replied the ghost.

The End

Although, as a ghost,
there really is no end is there?

If you ever come to Hoovington High School, you might see a ghost helping Maple protect the school from pranks.

It really is a strange sight!

The End

About the Author

Olivia Henderson

Olivia is a fabulously imaginative, bright and charismatic nine year old Dubai-based Author. At school, Olivia's favourite subject is Art and some of her favourite hobbies are swimming, sewing and drawing. In her spare time, she loves to hang out with her neighbours and have fun with her sisters and family.

To make the world a better place, Olivia wishes to encourage peace around the world through kindness.

Follow Olivia's publishing journey here,
www.youngauthoracademy.com/olivia-henderson

SCAN ME

Printed in Great Britain
by Amazon